FIRST PAGE

BENLIE THE ENGIE

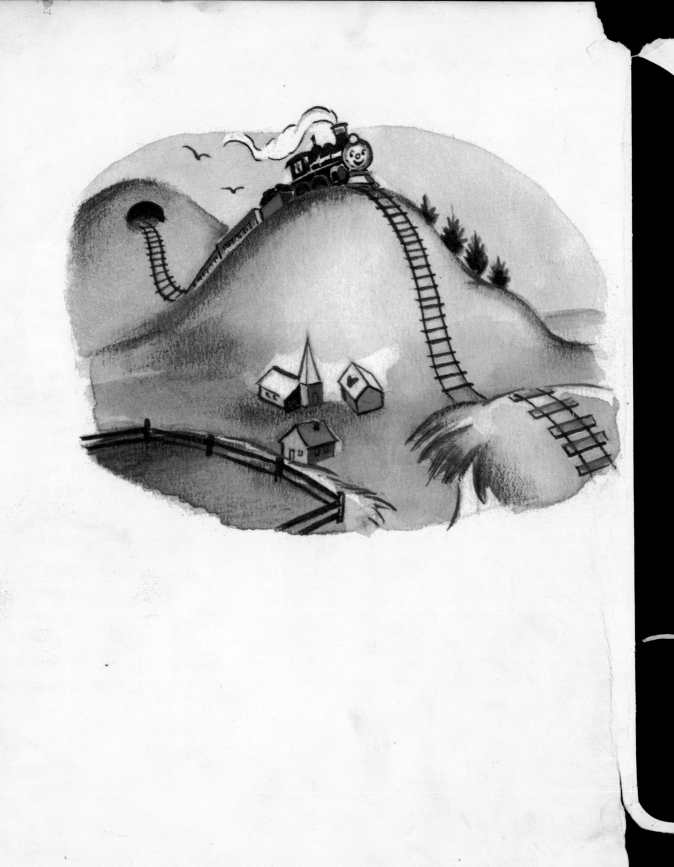

BENJIE ENGIE

By *LOUISE LAWRENCE DEVINE*

Illustrated by ELEANOR CORWIN

RAND McNALLY & COMPANY · Chicago

BENJIE ENGIE was a locomotive with a coal car, two passenger cars, and a baggage car fastened on behind.

And, unlike all the trains that Benjie Engie had ever known, he didn't have a single problem in the world to be sad about.

Benjie Engie made four trips each day between two big cities sixty miles apart, with twenty-seven stops at all the little towns along the way.

Some trains would have said, "I wish I were a Fast Through Train and did not have to stop twenty-seven times at all the little towns along the way! I wish I could be something besides a Slow Old Local!"

But not Benjie Engie. He never once said such a thing. He liked being a Slow Old Local, not because he was lazy, but because he liked to take things easy and enjoy life and look around and see things.

As he puffed along, he rolled his dreamy eyes from left to right and never missed a single thing. He watched birds fly, and clouds float, and cows munch grass, and bees buzz about, and sheep lie on the hill-sides in the shade of apple trees. He looked at bridges, and houses, and rivers.

One morning, as Benjie Engie left the roundhouse for his first run, he heard the engineer say to the fireman:

"Well, this is the last day that we will make the Local Run. Benjie Engie is going to be a Fast Through Train and go halfway across the United States with just four short stops. No more of these Slow Old Local trips for us!"

"OOH HOO!" snorted Benjie with a short sharp toot of his whistle. "I wonder how I'm going to like that!"

The next day the workmen started to work on Benjie. They squirted oil all over his insides and

gave him a new engine, two new wheels, and three coats of paint. In just a few days he roared out of the roundhouse with his new engine, turning his wheels faster than they had ever turned before. His whistle screeched and he click-clacked over

the rails so fast that he couldn't
count a single railroad tie as they
whizzed by under his cowcatcher.

Away from the city, out into the
country, he chuggapuffed.

Zip! past a town he went without
even slowing down.

Zip! through another town he flew, but he was going so fast that he didn't dare take his eyes off the track, so he didn't see anything but a great big

BLUR-R-R-R

as he went past.

He tried to look at something that seemed to be cows, but *Zip!* they were just BLURS as they whizzed by.

He tried rolling his eyes fast enough to see something that looked like a house, but it was just a BLUR as he roared by.

Everything——boys, bridges, clouds, girls, rivers, birds, and bees, were just BLURS as he went racing along,

hardly daring to look to the right or to the left.

"Whoo!" snorted Benjie Engie. "I just DON'T LIKE THIS AT ALL!"

But, because he knew he had a job to do, he made the trip halfway across the United States and tried hard to be happy about it, but, now,

Benjie was just like all the other trains he had ever known.

He had a PROBLEM IN LIFE and he was very, very sad.

Then one *very* sad day Benjie found that he couldn't remember what ANYTHING LOOKED LIKE!!!!!!

HOUSE-BLURS LOOKED LIKE BUGGY-BLURS.

CLOUD-BLURS LOOKED LIKE BOY-BLURS.

COW-BLURS LOOKED LIKE RIVER-BLURS.

BEE-BLURS LOOKED LIKE BRIDGE-BLURS.

TREE-BLURS LOOKED LIKE HORSE-BLURS.

GIRL-BLURS LOOKED LIKE AUTO-BLURS.

Even the railroad ties that Benjie Engie loved so much were just one big BLUR-R-R-R after another.

So Benjie made smoke-pictures for himself as he roared along.

"Now this is what
a cow looks like,"
he thought.

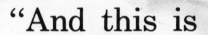

"And this is

a house.

"Here is
a doll buggy.

"And this is
a horse.

"Here is
a cloud.   "And this,
I am sure,
is a bee.

"No!" screeched Benjie with his whistle full of tears. "I don't want just to remember one thing from another! ! ! ! ! I want to really *see* them again."

Benjie got so unhappy that his whistle wouldn't blow right. He coughed and spluttered and cried big steamy tears. They ran down and rusted important levers, which made his wheels turn wobbly.

"What is wrong with Benjie Engie?" asked the engineer.

"I never saw him act this way before," said the fireman with a worried frown.

Then one day Benjie Engie's whistle wouldn't blow at all. His wheels wouldn't turn, and he could not puff out so much as a thimbleful of steam or smoke.

The president and vice-president of the railroad, and the engineer and the fireman, went out to the roundhouse and stood and looked at Benjie.

"Benjie Engie is not the locomotive he used to be," said the president of the railroad. "We had better put him in the roundhouse for a few days and see if we can get him to go again. And then," said the president slowly, "we shall have to put him back on the Slow Old Local Run. That is all he is good for now."

Benjie Engie wanted to jump up and down and kick his wheels together, but he didn't dare. He groaned loudly as another locomotive pulled him into the roundhouse.

The workmen hammered and banged and took the two new wheels off and put the old ones on

again. They took out the new engine
and gave the old one back to Benjie.
Then they squirted oil inside and
out until Benjie was a shiny, greasy,
happy mess.

The very next day Benjie Engie
went back to the Slow Old Local

Run. He had to remember not to toot too loudly or act too frisky for fear of being made a Fast Through Train again.

Benjie Engie was once again a happy, healthy train, for now he didn't have a PROBLEM IN LIFE anymore. From one big city to the other big city sixty miles away, with twenty-seven stops along the way,

Benjie Engie took his time and rolled along.

He saw bridges,

rivers,

bees,

houses,

boys on
bicycles.

men driving autos,

women
hanging up
clothes,

and little girls

pushing
doll buggies
around.

Once again everything was as it should be and not just one hurrying, scurrying, whirring, whizzing, zipping BLUR after another.

"WHOOOOOT!" tooted Benjie on his whistle.

He looked down at the shining rails, and on his four trips that day counted 720,000 railroad ties as they went by under his smiling cowcatcher! ! !

U. S. 1032201

STATION

LAST PAGE

BENLIE THE ENGIE